ISBN 0 86112 724 2
Published by Brimax Books Ltd, Newmarket, England. 1991.
Reprinted 1993
Printed in Portugal.

MY FIRST STORYBOOK

Illustrated by Stephanie Ryder

Brimax Books · Newmarket · England

Animal Noises

by Iris Smart

Trump like an elephant,
Growl like a grizzly bear,
Roar and claw like a lion
Springing from its lair.

Chatter like the monkeys do
Swinging from the trees,
Splash and spout like a whale
Swimming in the sea.

Growl and snarl like a tiger,
Snort like buffalo do,
Laugh like a laughing hyena,
Squawk like a cockatoo.

Grunt and snort like a wart hog,
Hiss and twist like a snake,
See how many animal sounds
And noises you can make.

Bojo's Waggly Tail
by Frances Kendle

Bojo the puppy was always getting into mischief.
His big, floppy paws kept walking in his dinner, and when he had a drink, his tongue splashed water everywhere. But Bojo's biggest problem was his waggly tail. It was always knocking things over.

CRASH! went the vase when Bojo was looking out of the window. SPLOSH! went the goldfish bowl as the waggly tail hit the table.
The little goldfish was saved in time, but Bojo just didn't know how to stop his tail from wagging.

"I wish you would keep still," Bojo said to his tail, but it didn't take any notice. Suddenly Bojo had an idea. "I'll catch my tail and hold it still," he said.
Round and round in circles he went, first one way and then the other, but he just couldn't catch his tail!

Then Bojo noticed Ming the cat asleep on a chair.

"She has a long tail," said Bojo. "But it doesn't wag all the time."

He decided to ask Ming why.

"Excuse me, Ming," said Bojo, "But why doesn't your tail wag like mine?"

Ming opened one eye.

"It does if I want it to," she said and she gave it an angry swish.

"But how do you keep your tail still?" asked Bojo. "If I break anything else today, I'm not allowed to have any dinner," he said sadly.

Ming was a very sly cat.

"If you let me share your dinner with you, I'll sit on your tail and keep it still," she purred.

Bojo wasn't very happy with that but he agreed.

Ming stood up and stretched and jumped down onto Bojo's tail. She curled up and went back to sleep. Bojo must have slept too, because the next thing he heard was his dinner bowl rattling in the kitchen. Bojo and Ming rushed into the kitchen for something to eat.

Ming licked her lips when she saw Bojo's bowl of meat. But she had forgotten that puppies always wag their tails when they are happy and Bojo was very happy that it was dinner time. His tail wagged so hard that it knocked Ming into his bowl of water!

"Atishoo!" sneezed Ming.
Water dripped from her nose
and whiskers. "Atishoo!"
Bojo started to laugh.
Ming looked a very funny
sight indeed. And he decided
that having a waggly tail
wasn't so bad, afterall!

Toby's Good Turn

by Mae Cheeseman

Toby was in a helpful mood. "Have you any jobs for me to do?" he asked his mother. So she let him do the washing up. But Toby dropped a plate on the floor.

"Why don't you tidy your bedroom instead," said Mother.

So Toby folded his clothes and made his bed, but that didn't take very long. Toby wandered into the garden. His father was in the shed practising his trumpet for a concert that evening. "Have you any jobs for me to do, Dad?" asked Toby.

"Let me think," said Dad.
"You could polish this trumpet
while I fetch my suit for
tonight's concert."
So Toby was given the duster
and polish. He began to
polish the trumpet as hard
as he could, but it didn't
look very shiny.

"I know what to do," said Toby. He carried the trumpet into the house and ran upstairs to the bathroom. Toby filled the sink with warm, soapy water and began to wash the trumpet. Soon the trumpet was covered in bubbles.

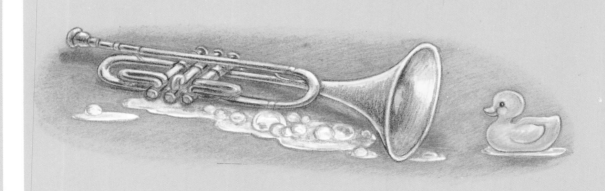

Toby rubbed the trumpet dry
and ran back down to the shed.
He polished the trumpet until
it gleamed.
Dad was very pleased when he
arrived home.
"Well done, Toby," he said.

That evening at the concert, Toby watched as Dad played the trumpet. Suddenly, there was a strange gurgling noise and lots of bright, shiny bubbles floated out of the trumpet and into the crowd! Everyone began to laugh. And even Dad smiled when he realised how Toby had made the trumpet so shiny!

Dorabelle's New Hat

by June Hammond

Dorabelle Donkey pulled her blue cart into the farmyard. Inside was a basket of carrots and a bunch of flowers.

"Hello, Sam," said Dorabelle sadly to Sam the sheepdog. "I am going to the fair."

"Why are you so sad?" asked Sam.

"There will be a prize for the prettiest hat," said Dorabelle. "And I can't find one to wear."

"We can ask Daisy Duck,"
said Sam.
Daisy Duck was swimming on
the pond.
"I cannot help you," said Daisy.
"We can ask Charlie Cat."
Charlie Cat was in the barn.
"I know where to find a hat,"
he said to his friends.

Everyone followed Charlie Cat into the farmer's field.
"There is a hat," said Charlie.
Dorabelle saw an old tattered hat sitting on a scarecrow.
"I can't wear that," she said.
"Everyone will laugh at me."

Sam, Daisy and Charlie didn't know what to do. They climbed into Dorabelle's little cart to think. Dorabelle pulled the cart up a steep hill, then stopped to rest. As she shook off her harness, the little blue cart began to roll backwards. "Stop!" everyone shouted.

The little cart raced down the hill and into a field.
Dorabelle ran after it as fast as she could.
Crash! Dorabelle and the cart bumped into a big haystack.
Sam, Daisy and Charlie landed in a heap on top of Dorabelle!

"You have found your hat," said Daisy Duck to Dorabelle. Then Dorabelle saw that the basket in her cart had lost its carrots and was sitting on her head!

"We can decorate it with the flowers," said Sam. Dorabelle was very happy. She was the best looking donkey at the fair. And sure enough, she won first prize for the prettiest hat!

The Little Bear Who Lost His Hat
by Saviour Pirotta

Once there was a little bear who had a pirate suit and hat. One windy day his mother said, "Put on your pirate suit, Little Bear and I'll make you a pirate cake with a chocolate treasure chest inside." Little Bear went to change. But as he was putting on his hat, the wind blew it out of the window.

Little Bear ran into the garden, but he couldn't see his hat. Just then, a penguin sped by on a skateboard.

"Where are you going, Little Bear?" asked the penguin.

"I'm chasing my hat," said Little Bear.

"A skateboard is faster than a pair of paws," said the penguin. "Would you like a lift?"

The penguin and Little Bear skated to the end of the path. They couldn't catch the hat. Just then a hippo rode by on a bicycle.

"Where are you going?" he asked.

"We are chasing my hat," said Little Bear.

"A bicycle is faster than a skateboard," said the hippo. So they all cycled to the end of the lane. But they still couldn't catch the hat.

Just then a tiger sped by in a sports car.
"Where are you all going?" he asked.
"We are chasing my hat," said Little Bear.
"A sports car is much faster than a bicycle," said the tiger.
So they all drove to the end of the road, but they still couldn't catch the hat.

Just then, an elephant drove
by in a train.
"Where are you going?"
she asked.
"We are chasing my hat,"
said Little Bear.
"A train is much faster than
a car," said the elephant.
So they rode in the train
until they reached the sea.
But they still couldn't catch
the hat.

At last a monkey flew by in a plane.
"Where are you going?" he asked.
"We are chasing my hat," said Little Bear.
"A plane is much faster than a train," said the monkey.
So they all flew out to sea.

Little Bear looked down at
the sea. A fish was eating
his pirate hat.
"I've lost my hat!" he cried.
"And I've missed my tea."
"I can get you home in time
for tea," said the monkey.
He turned the plane around
and flew back towards land.
Little Bear saw hills and
rivers and kings' castles
as small as match boxes.

At last Little Bear saw his house. He flew out of the plane on a pink parachute. "Where have you been?" asked his mother.

"I've been to sea," said Little Bear.

He washed his paws and sat down to tea. He cut the cake and there inside the chocolate treasure chest was a brand new pirate hat with an icing sugar skull and cross bones!

Rip Rap Rop
by Iris Smart

Rip Rap Rop,
Three little mice in a shop,
A shop full of things to eat.
They got in the store
Through a hole in the floor,
Squickety squackety squeak.

They nibbled the cookies,
Nibbled the bread,
Nibbled the cakes and the pies;
While keeping a look out
For Tiddles the cat
With their sharp, beady eyes.

They nibbled the sausage,
Nibbled the ham,
The three little hungry mice;
They nibbled the cheese
And how they did sneeze when
They upset the sugar and spice!

Rip Rap Rop,
Three little mice in a shop,
A shop full of things to eat.
After cleaning their whiskers
and licking their paws
They all fell fast asleep!

Willie Weasel Finds a Job

by Diane Jackman

Willie Weasel was learning to play the guitar. All the other animals in Barton Wood went about with cotton wool in their ears to block out the noise. Soon the woodland store ran out of cotton wool and Willie's playing became even louder.

Then he began to sing, too,
which was even worse.
"Please stop, Willie!"
pleaded all the animals.
But Willie kept on playing
and singing.
"Why don't you take up
a quiet hobby?" asked Owl.
"Stamp collecting would
be very good."

"This isn't just a hobby,"
said Willie. "I will find
a job playing my guitar.
You just wait until I'm
rich and famous."
And he twanged the guitar
strings and added an extra
verse to his song.

One day a notice appeared on the big oak tree in the middle of Barton Wood. WANTED: GUITAR PLAYER FOR THE WOODLAND BAND. MEET AT THE BANDSTAND AT NOON. Willie rushed off to the bandstand to wait.

But when Sammy Squirrel
the bandmaster heard
Willie play, he said,
"I'm very sorry, Willie,
but I don't think you
will ever get a job playing
your guitar."
But he was wrong.
The next day, Mr Badger
came to visit Willie.

"I've heard you playing your guitar," Mr Badger said to Willie. "Would you like to come and work for me instead?"

"Oh, yes please!" cried Willie happily.

"You can play and sing as loudly as you like," said Mr Badger, smiling. "That way you will scare the crows away from my lettuces every day!"

Suzie's Tree

by Diane Jackman

In the middle of Suzie's garden stood a very old tree. It had strong branches to climb on and a hollow in the trunk big enough to hide in. Suzie loved to play in her tree. One night there was a terrible storm. Suzie lay in bed listening to the wind and the rain.

In the morning, Suzie looked out of her window. There were leaves and broken branches lying on the grass. Her tree had been split in two by the storm. One half lay on the grass and the other still stood upright in the ground.

Suzie ran to tell Dad.
She was very sad. She went
into the garden and put her
arms around the trunk of
her tree. The next day,
Dad cut down what was left
of the tree then sawed up
all the wood and piled it
near the garden shed.

One day, Suzie came home from school and saw all the wood had gone. Dad was busy in the shed, sawing and hammering loudly.
"What are you making?" asked Suzie.
"Oh, this and that," said Dad with a secret smile.

On Suzie's birthday, Dad
woke her early.
"Look out of the window,"
he said.
There, in the middle of
the garden, where Suzie's
tree once stood was
a wooden climbing frame.
It had bars, a ladder and
a swinging rope.
"So that is what you were
making!" cried Suzie.

Suzie quickly dressed and
ran into the garden.
She climbed up the wooden
ladder and onto the climbing
frame. She waved to Dad
as she slid down the rope.
"It's great, Dad," she said.
"Just like having my own
tree again!"

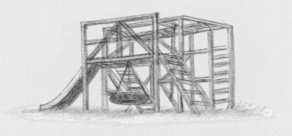